Sink the Tirpitz

by

Jim Eldridge

Illustrated by Dylan Gibson

To my wife, Lynne

With special thanks to:

James Butler
Shane Walker
Tom Wiltshire

First published in 2010 in Great Britain by
Barrington Stoke Ltd
18 Walker St, Edinburgh, EH3 7LP

www.barringtonstoke.co.uk

ISBN: 978-1-84299-756-7

Printed in Great Britain by Bell & Bain Ltd

Contents

Chapter 1
Attack!

June 1942. The night was cold and dark. As the waves of the freezing North Sea rose and fell, the convoy of ships rocked up and down. There were 30 ships in the convoy: six Royal Navy destroyers and the rest merchant ships, taking supplies that were badly needed from Britain to Russia.

This was the Arctic. The sea was so cold that if a man fell into it he would die in just a few minutes.

Fog hung over the sea. Somewhere out in that fog *it* was hiding. The deadly danger. The *Tirpitz*, the huge German battleship. It weighed 43,000 tons and was half a mile long. It could destroy a whole convoy.

Suddenly an alarm rang out on the leading destroyer! A huge shape had been spotted on the radar. *Tirpitz* was out in the North Sea and was sailing towards the convoy! With her was a fleet of smaller German battleships, and subs known as

U-boats. The message was passed by radio

along the convoy.

"Split up!" came the next radio message. "Break up the convoy."

The hope was that if the ships of the convoy went off in different directions, then *Tirpitz* wouldn't be able to attack them all.

The destroyers headed into the thick fog towards the huge shape on their radar screens. As the ships scattered, other shapes rose up from far down in the sea. These were the German U-boats. They were hidden by the fog, but the U-boats could see their victims on their own radar. They were like a pack of killer hunting dogs.

Each U-boat picked its target and went after it.

The ships of the convoy saw the U-boats on their own radar, but it was too late to defend against them.

Woooooshhhhhh! The sound of torpedoes
racing through the water could be heard all
over the ships.

KA-BOOOOOOMMMMMM!!!!

The night sky lit up red and yellow as a ship blew up when the torpedo hit it. Then another ship blew up.

Thick black oily smoke mixed in with the fog. Oil on the sea burned. Men in the water yelled for help, but were pulled down by the icy sea, or burnt by the flames.

More torpedoes. More fire and loud blasts. More black smoke mixing with the freezing fog.

The convoy was sunk.

Chapter 2
Sink the Tirpitz!

In the War Room in London the mood was grim. Everyone was silent. Admiral Smith pointed to the map on the wall. It showed the North Sea between Britain and the port of Murmansk in north Russia.

"This is the route the convoys have to take to get supplies to the Russians,"

Admiral Smith said to the other men. "The Russians are fighting Hitler and the Germans. They need the supplies we send them if they are to beat them. In the last few months most of our convoys have been sunk when they were attacked by German U-boats and German warships.

"The problem is that the German ships are protected by the huge German battleship, the *Tirpitz*. It can fire missiles from a long way away. It can hit our battleships before we can get in range. If we don't sink the *Tirpitz*, our convoys will all be sunk."

"What about bombing *Tirpitz* from planes?" asked an RAF Commander.

Admiral Smith shook his head.

"*Tirpitz* has very long-range anti-aircraft guns. Any plane trying to attack it when it's at sea would be shot down long before it reached the ship."

"Why don't we attack it when it's not in action?" said another RAF man. "We can bomb it when it's not at sea."

Again, Admiral Smith shook his head.

"When it's not at sea, *Tirpitz* is kept safe in a Norwegian fjord, which is a long narrow arm of the sea. This fjord has high cliff walls on all sides which protect the ship. The Germans have big guns all round the tops of the cliffs. Because of the cliffs and these guns, no bomber can get near enough to drop its bombs on the *Tirpitz*."

"Why not use subs?" asked another Admiral. "Send a sub into the fjord and torpedo it."

"We have tried that," said Admiral Smith. "The Germans have put anti-submarine nets across the mouth of the fjord. This anti-submarine net is made of metal so it also stops torpedoes getting past. There is also a floating mine-field at the entrance to the fjord, which is only lifted when the *Tirpitz* is going out into open sea. Any submarine attack on the *Tirpitz* while it is in the fjord will fail.

"So, gentlemen: we can't beat it in a battle at sea. We can't sink it by using aeroplanes or submarines. But if we don't destroy the *Tirpitz* we will lose this war!"

One of the Navy scientists started to speak. Everyone looked at him.

"I've got an idea," he said. "We could try mini subs."

The RAF commander laughed.

"No good at all!" he said. "Mini subs are too small to make it across the North Sea and back. The crew would be doomed to die!"

"Yes," nodded the naval scientist. "That's what I think will happen."

Chapter 3
The Mini Subs

The inside of the mini sub was the size of a very very small room. The four men of the crew sat and looked at one another. They could not stand up in there.

"I've been in bigger phone boxes," said Bob Gray.

The other three nodded.

Bob, the skipper, sat in the middle of the sub next to the periscope. Sam, the navigator, sat next to him. Fred, the engineer, sat behind them at the controls for the pump and the motors. Joe, the diver, sat next to the door to the tiny chamber which led out to the water.

There were four mini subs on the mission. They had been towed by larger subs across the North Sea. When they were near the coast of Norway, the crews left the large subs and got into the small ones.

The subs were so small there was no room even for a radio. There was one tiny periscope. There were three windows, one in the top and one at each side. Fuel and the batteries were at the front of the sub. The engines were at the back.

Outside, a large bomb was fixed to each side of the sub. Each bomb had two tons of explosives. When levers inside the sub were pulled these bombs would be dropped and sink to the sea bed. This meant the tiny sub

had to get right beneath the *Tirpitz* before

it dropped the bombs.

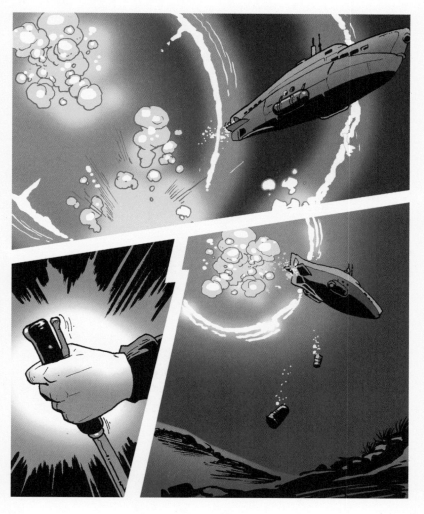

The plan was for the mini subs to find their way past the floating mines that protected the entry to the fjord. When they reached the anti-sub net at the entry to the fjord, the diver was to swim out and cut the metal net so the mini sub could get past. The sub was to make for the *Tirpitz* and drop the bombs under it; then try to get away to safety before the bombs blew up.

Each sub was taking a different route past the minefield and the net. If only one of them got past there was a chance the mission would succeed. But there was also a chance they would all die.

Chapter 4
Minefield

"Mines ahead!" said Bob.

Using the periscope, he could see them floating on the water in front of them. The minefield stretched right across the entry to the fjord. The mines were fixed by strong wires to weights. There was only one way through the minefield, and that was to zig-zag between the wires. If they bumped up against a wire, it would bang the mine against the sub and they would die.

"Slow as you can," said Bob to Fred, the engineer.

Fred cut the speed as far down as he could.

"Slow left," said Bob.

Sam, the navigator, steered the sub to the left. Bob kept his eyes to the periscope, working out a path past the maze of wires.

The only way to get past was by going very slow. The problem was that they only had enough oxygen for six hours. If they went too slow they wouldn't have time to get back through the minefield after they'd dropped the bombs.

Slowly, moving left and right, the mini sub made its way past the minefield. It took them 30 minutes of slow zig-zagging to get through.

What are the other mini subs doing? Bob was thinking. There were no shock waves of explosions, so he guessed none of them had hit a mine yet.

They got past the minefield, and at once Bob saw a curtain of chains hanging down in front of them.

"Stop motor!" he called.

Fred stopped the motor.

"OK, Joe," said Bob. "This is your job."

Joe had his wet suit and oxygen cylinders on. He put on his oxygen mask and went into the tiny chamber. Fred closed the water-tight door shut behind him.

Joe let the small room fill with water, then he opened the outside hatch and swam out.

He got to the huge wire net. He took a pair of wire cutters from his belt and began to cut from the bottom of the net up. It was hard work. Because the water was freezing cold he had to wear thick gloves, which made the work even harder.

At last Joe had made a cut in the net big enough for the mini sub to get through. He pulled the cut parts of the net up and fixed them so the sub could get through without getting tangled up in the loose ends of the net.

He signalled back to the mini sub, which began to move forward. It just made it through the gap. The sub stopped, and Joe swam to the sub, opened the hatch, and got back inside.

Next stop, *Tirpitz*!

Chapter 5
Explosions Under Water!

Bob kept his eyes fixed to the periscope as the mini sub went slowly forward. Then he saw it! The bottom of the *Tirpitz*! It was about two miles away.

"We're almost there, boys!" he said. He was very excited.

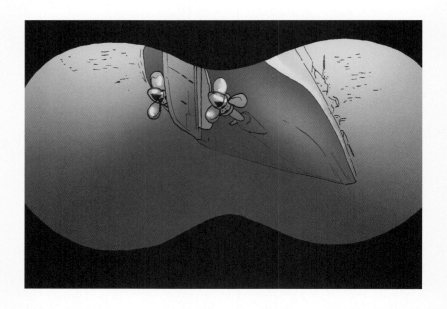

Suddenly there was the sound of a loud blast. It was muffled by the water, but they all felt the shock wave hit their mini sub.

The blast had come from behind them. One of the other mini subs must have blown up.

"They must have hit a mine," said Fred.

They all knew what that meant. The blast would have set off the mini sub's bombs.

"The Germans will have heard that," said Sam. "They'll be watching out for us now."

"Then let's get our bombs down quick!" said Bob. "Full speed ahead!"

As they moved faster through the water, they felt another shock wave from behind them, and again heard the dull sound of an explosion.

"That could be the Germans dropping depth charges," said Joe.

But they also knew it could have been another of the mini subs blowing up.

They were nearly at the *Tirpitz* now.

"Take us lower, Sam," said Bob.

"We'll be scraping the sea bottom," said Sam.

"Better to scrape that than scrape the *Tirpitz* and alert the Germans," said Bob.

They brought the sub right beneath the giant battleship.

"Right," said Bob. "Set the timers for 40
minutes."

Fred set the timers on the bombs so that
they would explode in 40 minutes. That
should give them time to get back through

the hole in the net, and through the floating minefield.

"Done," he said.

"Right. Bombs away," said Bob.

Joe and Fred pulled a lever each, and the two large bombs were dropped and sank down.

"OK," said Bob. "Let's get out of here!"

Chapter 6
Caught!

The mini sub raced away from the *Tirpitz* towards the hole in the wire net.

"Go slow through the hole," Bob told Fred as he watched through the periscope.

Slowly the mini sub crept forward. Suddenly there was the sound of scraping metal from outside, and then the sub stopped.

"We've got trapped in the net!" said Sam. "It's been let down. Either the Germans have done that ..."

"... Or the blasts made it drop," finished Bob.

He turned to Joe.

"Joe, you've got to get out there and cut a bigger hole for us, or we're stuck here. And when those bombs go off ..."

"Leave it to me, skipper," said Joe.

He put on his oxygen tanks and mask as fast as he could and went back into the small room. Five minutes had gone by. Fred slammed the water-tight door shut. Bob, Sam and Fred looked out of the window and saw Joe swim out and swim up to the roof of the sub. They heard scraping sounds from the metal net as Joe started cutting it. All

eyes were on the clock. Eight minutes gone!
Nine minutes!

"We're not going to make it," said Sam.

Another minute passed. Then Joe was
there at the window giving them the thumbs
up sign. He'd done it.

41

"OK! Forward!" said Bob. "Keep as low as you can. And slow!"

Slowly the small sub crept forward.

When they had got past the net there were just 25 minutes left before the bombs they had dropped under the *Tirpitz* went off. And they still had to get back through the minefield, which had taken them half an hour coming the other way!

Chapter 7
The Bombs Go Off

All their eyes were on the clock as they entered the minefield.

"Fast as you can," Bob said to Fred.

"Not too fast, skipper," warned Sam. "If we hit one of these mines we're dead."

"If we don't get through the minefield before our bombs go off, we could be dead as well," said Bob.

They moved forward, zig-zagging like before, only this time going as fast as they dared.

Suddenly there was the sound of scraping from beneath them.

"We're too low!" said Bob. "Bring us up, Sam!"

"I can't," said Sam. "If we do we'll be too close to the mines."

With a shock, Bob saw what must have
happened.

"The tide's going out!" he said. "The
mines are sinking lower in the water!"

"If we scrape along the bottom, the
Germans might hear us," warned Sam.

"If we blow up they are quite sure to hear us," said Bob. "We've got to take the risk! Stay low and go as fast as you can!"

The mini sub zig-zagged between the wires and the mines, scraping along the bottom of the fjord all the way. All the time the clock kept ticking: 37 minutes, 38, 39. Just as they passed the final row of mines ...

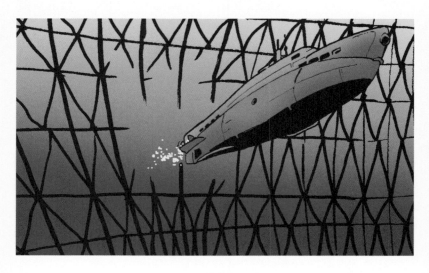

KARBOOOMMMMMMM!!

A huge blast from behind them pushed them forward. Then there was another blast.

"Chain re-action!" yelled Bob. "Our bombs must have set off the ship's own ammunition! She's blowing up! We've done it! We've sunk the *Tirpitz*!"

The Real History

In 1943 the huge German battleship
Tirpitz attacked and sank the supply lines in
the North Sea between Britain and Russia.
All attempts to sink the *Tirpitz* failed: at
sea, no Royal Navy ships were a match for
the great ship. When not at sea, the *Tirpitz*
was kept in a fjord in Norway. The high cliff
walls around the fjord prevented attack by
planes. The shallow entrance to the fjord

made it impossible to attack by submarine. Anti-torpedo nets had been placed at the entrance to the fjord, giving the *Tirpitz* further protection. There seemed no way the *Tirpitz* could be put out of action, until a small fleet of six mini subs called X-Craft, each with a crew of four men, were sent on a mission to sink it. Two of the X-Craft were lost on the trip over to Norway. Of the four who got to Norway, only two managed to set off explosive charges beneath the *Tirpitz*, which crippled it.

In this story, the crew of one of the X-craft get away. In fact, the crews of both X-craft were taken by the Germans and made prisoner.

The *Tirpitz* was so badly damaged in the attack it never took part in any sea battles again. It was moved to another fjord in Norway where it was at last destroyed by RAF bombers in 1944.

The Dunkirk Escape

by
Jim Eldridge

Dave Jones is trapped on the beach at
Dunkirk, as bombs explode all around him.
Can his son Tom get there in time to
save him?

You can order *The Dunkirk Escape* from our website at
www.barringtonstoke.co.uk

The Dancing Stones

by
Maggie Pearson

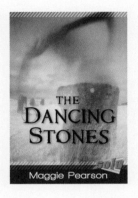

They say if you dance round the stones at midnight you'll be turned to stone.
Kelly thinks it's rubbish, and she's going to prove it. But Ben's worried. What if she's wrong?

You can order *The Dancing Stones* from our website at www.barringtonstoke.co.uk

Under Cover of Darkness

by
Pat Thomson

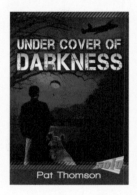

The Nazis have arrived in Michel's village.
But the Resistance are fighting back. Can
Michel help to win the secret war?

You can order *Under Cover of Darkness* from our website at
www.barringtonstoke.co.uk

They Shall Not Pass

by

Andy Croft

Sam is Jewish. His friend Alf is Irish. At first that didn't matter. But now the Black Shirts want to get rid of the Jews – and Alf is on their side. Now Sam has to fight for what's right ...

You can order *They Shall Not Pass* from our website at www.barringtonstoke.co.uk